Ike & Mike Magical Storybook Adventure

First Tour of Washington DC

Published by Foxey World Publishing

Division of The Friends of Rick Daniels Inc.

731 Jefferson ST NW Washington, DC 20011 USA

(202) 722-0502 / www.thefriendsofrickdaniels.com

Published in the United States of America

Children's Fiction

Acknowledgment

I would like to thank the children from The Children's Hut Daycare at 510 Kennedy ST NW. Every day they would walk up my street on the 700th block of Jefferson ST NW, and sit on the wall of the church, across the street from my house. Every day I would read them a book, until one day, I ran out of books. They asked me to tell them a story. I started making up stories about Ike & Mike, two stuffed pups that sit on the back of my sofa. The children fell in love with the Ike & Mike stories, and I knew then, to put Ike & Mike into print.

I would also like to thank my mom and dad, whom I miss so much; you always believed in me. I dedicate the Ike & Mike series of books to you.

To Minnie Green, my neighbor and good friend for so many years, whom I also miss very much. I also dedicate this book to you.

A very special thanks to Ben's Chili Bowl

I would like to thank Virginia Ali and her son Nizam Ali for supporting me in all my adventures. You also believed in me from day one with my first book, Little Remy. Thank you for your support.

To my tutor Melissa Wilks. Since you've became my tutor, you have opened doors I never knew were possible for me. Thank you so much.

Rick Daniels

In a house on the 700th block of Jefferson ST NW, Ike & Mike are two stuffed pups. They live there with all their animal friends. This is no ordinary house. In this house there is

MAGIC!

There's a secret to make the magic begin. All you have to do is close your eyes and say:

"Come to life, Ike!
Come to life, Mike!"

They will come alive in an amazing magical storybook adventure.

Ever since Ike and Mike arrived at the house on Jefferson ST NW, all they do is sit on the back of a sofa with the rest of their animal friends.

One day, Ike tells his older brother Mike, "I'm tired of sitting on this sofa. All we do is sit!"

Mike asks, "Well, what would you like to do Ike?"

Ike says, "Let's tour DC!"

Mike says, "Great! We can go see the Washington Monument, the Jefferson Memorial, the Lincoln Memorial, and the Martin Luther King Jr. Memorial!"

Ike asks his older brother Mike,
    "How will we get around DC?"

Mike says, "We'll take the bus. Spell
    bus Ike."

"B-U-S!"

Mike says, "That's right. Great job Ike!"

Mike says, "We'll have to catch the
E4 bus on the corner of 8th & Kennedy
ST NW, then transfer to the 79
express bus on Georgia Ave and
Kennedy ST. Spell bus again Ike."

"B-U-S!"

"Right again Ike! Great job!"

The E4 bus finally arrives.

When the two enter the bus they say,

" Hello Mr. Bus Driver!"

The bus driver, being a bear says,
"Growl! Growl! Growl!"

Ike says, "We're going to tour DC!"

The bus driver says, "That's great,
now please take a seat."

Mike says, "Spell bear Ike."

"B-E-A-R!"

"Great job Ike!"

Ike sits next to a pig, and the pig says,
"Oink! Oink! Oink!"

Ike tells the pig, "We're going to tour DC!"

The pig says, "That's great!"

Mike says, "Spell pig Ike,"

"P-I-G!"

"That's right! Great job Ike!"

Mike sits next to a turkey, and the turkey says,

"Gobble! Gobble! Gobble!"

Mike tells the turkey, "We're going to see some famous memorials."

The turkey says, "That's great!"

Ike asks Mike, "Can you spell turkey?"

"T-U-R-K-E-Y!"

Ike says, "You're smart Mike! That word is too hard for me."

After a short ride on the E4 bus, they transfer to the 79 Express.

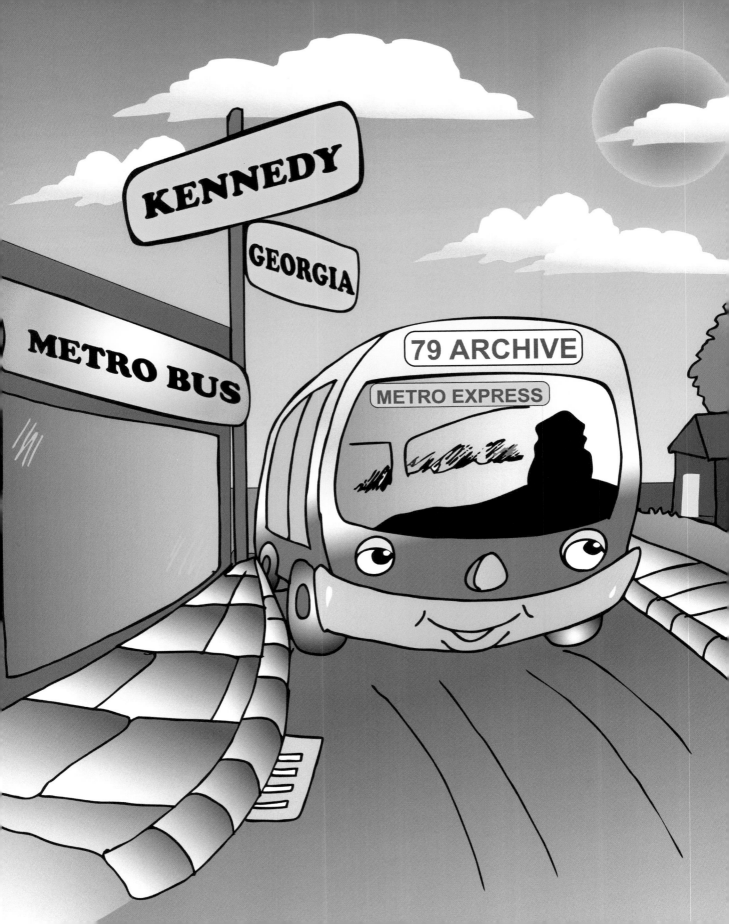

When they get on the 79 bus they say,

"Hi Mr. Bus Driver!"

The driver being a horse says,

"Neigh! Neigh! Neigh!"

They tell the bus driver, "We're going

to tour DC!"

The bus driver says, "That's great!

Now please take a seat."

Ike asks Mike, "Can you spell horse?"

"H-O-R-S-E!"

Ike says, "You're a great speller Mike."

Ike sits next to a cat and the cat says,
"Meow! Meow! Meow!"

Ike tells the cat, "We're going to tour DC!"

The cat says, "That's great!"

Mike says, "Spell cat Ike."

Ike says, "That is an easy one!"

"C-A-T!"

Mike says, "Good job Ike!"

Mike sits next to a cow and the cow says,
"Moo! Moo! Moo!"

Mike tells the cow, "We're going to see
some famous memorials!"

The cow says, "That's great!"

Mike says, "Spell cow."

"C-O-W!"

"Good job Ike!"

After a long ride on the 79 Express bus, they arrive at 7th & Constitution Ave. The two get off the bus to find the famous memorials. Not knowing which way to go, they decide to ask a policeman.

Mike tells the policeman, "We have come to see some famous memorials. Which way should we go?"

The policeman being a lion says,
"Roar! Roar! Roar!
There that way!"
Ike and Mike say, "Thank you!"

Mike says, "Spell lion."

"L-I-O-N!"

"Great job Ike!"

Ike & Mike's first stop is the Washington Monument.

Ike tells Mike, "I can climb it!"

Mike says, "Don't-you-dare!"

Ike says, "You're not the boss of me!"

Mike says, "But I'm the oldest!"

Ike says, "Yeah, by only one minute! Watch me!" And up he goes.

Everyone is yelling:

"Get down, Ike!!!"
"Get down, Ike!!!"

Right before everyone's eyes, Ike falls.

Mike runs over to Ike,
"Are you OK!?"

Ike says, "I'm OK."

Mike tells him, "No- more- climbing!"

Rubbing his head, Ike says, "OK, I promise."

Their next stops are the

Jefferson and Lincoln Memorials.

Their final stop is the

Martin Luther King Jr. Memorial.

After a long day of visiting memorials, Ike tells Mike, "I'm hungry!"

Mike says, "Me too! Where would you like to eat?"

Ike says, "Hmm, let's go to Ben's Chili Bowl!"

Mike agrees and off they go.

Once they arrive at Ben's Chili Bowl,
a very nice wolf says,
"Awuoo! Awuoo! Awuoo!
Welcome to Ben's Chili Bowl, please
take a seat!"

Ike says, "Can you spell wolf?"

Mike says, "That's easy,
W-O-L-F-!"

Ike asks, "What are you going to order?"

Mike says, "I'm going to have a chili
dog, chili cheese fries, and a strawberry
shake."

Ike says, "I'll have the same thing."

A few minutes later, a duck brings their food. The duck says,

"Quack! Quack! Quack!"

Here's your food!"

Ike and Mike say, "Thank you!"

Ike asks Mike, "Can you spell duck?"

Mike says, "Sure."

D-U-C-K!"

Ike says, "You're a good speller, Mike."

Mike puts a napkin around his neck and begins to eat. Ike puts his chili fries on his chili dog, then stuffs them in his shake and slams it into his face!

Mike says, "Eww! Ike, what are you
    doing?! That's no way to eat!"

Ike says, "You're not the boss of me!"

Mike says, "But I'm the oldest!"

Ike says, "Only by one minute!"

Mike says, "I'm still the oldest and
    that means you should listen to me!"

So Mike helps his little brother clean up
and they start the long journey home.

After a long ride on the 79 Express, they arrive back home to the house on Jefferson ST. They take their place on the back of the sofa with the rest of their friends.

For now the magic is over, but if you want another story, remember what the secret is! All you have to do is close your eyes and say:

"Come to life, Ike! Come to life, Mike!"

Until their next magical storybook adventure.
Goodbye!

CPSIA information can be obtained at www.ICGtesting.com
Printed in the USA
BVIW12n1910160318
510612BV00004B/17